NAN AND THE SEA MONSTER

Copyright © 1990 American Teacher Publications

Copyright © 1989 American Teacher Publications
Published by Raintree Publishers Limited Partnership
All rights reserved. No part of this book may be reproduced or utilized in any form or
by any means, electronic or mechanical, including photocopying, recording, or by any
information storage and retrieval system without permission in writing. Inquiries should be
addressed to Raintree Publishers, 310 West Wisconsin Avenue,
Milwaukee, Wisconsin, 53203.

Library of Congress number: 89-3606

Library of Congress Cataloging in Publication Data

Dale, Nora
    Nan and the sea monster / Nora Dale; illustrated by Maria Pia Marrella.

    (Real readers)
    Summary: When Nan the mermaid looks at her friend Dolphin and thinks she sees
a sea monster, her friends realize that she needs glasses.
    [1. Mermaids—Fiction. 2. Eyeglasses—Fiction.] I. Marrella, Maria Pia, ill. II. Title.
III. Series.
PZ7.F33577Nan 1989   [E]—dc19   89-3606
ISBN: 0-8172-3526-4

    2 3 4 5 6 7 8 9 0   93 92 91 90

Nan and the Sea Monster

by Nora Dale
illustrated by Maria Pia Marrella

Raintree Publishers
Milwaukee

Nan was swimming in the sea when she saw one of her friends. "How are you, Crab?" said Nan.

"I'm fine, but I'm not Crab. I'm Starfish," said Starfish. "Can't you see that I have no shell?"

"Oops," said Nan. "I'm sorry, Starfish. I guess I didn't see you too well. Can we still be friends? Come and swim with me!"

Nan and Starfish were swimming in the sea when they saw one of their friends.

"How are you, Fish?" said Nan.

"I'm fine, but I'm not Fish. I'm Crab!" said Crab. "Can't you see that I have no fins?"

"Oops," said Nan. "I'm sorry, Crab. I guess I didn't see you too well. Can we still be friends? Come and swim with me!"

Nan, Starfish, and Crab were swimming in the sea when Nan thought she saw a good place to sit.

"Let's stop and sit on the rocks. I'll sit on this one," Nan said to her friends.

"I'm not a rock! I'm Turtle," said Turtle. "Can't you see that I have legs?"

"Oops," said Nan. "I'm sorry, Turtle. I guess I didn't see you too well. Can we still be friends? Come and swim with me!"

Just then Nan looked up and saw something move in the water.

"I see a tail! It's a big tail! It's the tail of a sea monster!" said Nan. "Look out! We must get away as fast as we can!"

And with that, Nan started to swim away as fast as she could.

"Wait!" called Crab and Starfish and Turtle.

Nan swam and swam.

When Nan looked back, she saw the sea monster following her in the water!

Nan was scared. She called to her friends for help.

Then the sea monster called to Nan.

"Stop! I am not a sea monster! Can't you see? I'm Dolphin!"

And so it was.

"Oops," said Nan. "I'm sorry, Dolphin, I guess I didn't see you too well. Can we still be friends? Come and swim with me!"

"That is one 'oops' too many," said Starfish.

"You scared all of us," said Turtle.

"You just can't see very well!" said Crab.

"We'll have to help you," said Turtle.

"I think I know who can help Nan," said Dolphin. "Follow me, everyone."

So Nan, Starfish, Crab, and Turtle all followed Dolphin. They swam until they came to a sign that said, "Dr. O's Place."

Dr. O's Place

"Well, hello," said Dr. O. "What can I do for you today?"

"My friend Nan thought I was a sea monster," said Dolphin.

"And she thought I was a rock," said Turtle.

"And that I was a fish," said Crab.

"And that I was a crab," said Starfish.

"So they think there is something wrong with my eyes," said Nan.

20

"Hmmm, let's see what we can see," Dr. O said.

First, Dr. O asked Nan to read some letters. Nan could not read the letters too well.

"Hmmm," Dr. O said. He used all his hands to put glass lenses in front of Nan's eyes. Nan looked through many lenses and read the letters.

Some of the lenses helped Nan see better. At last, Dr. O got just the right lenses for Nan. When Nan looked through two lenses, she read all the letters, just right.

"Aha! You need eyeglasses, Nan," Dr. O said. "I will make them for you."

ZIP! BOOM! BANG!

Dr. O used all his hands to make a pair of eyeglasses for Nan. They were very nice glasses indeed. The frames had seashells on them.

"Here, put them on," said Dr. O.

Nan put on her new glasses.

"Oh, I can see everything so well!" Nan said. "These eyeglasses are great! But how do I look? Will everyone laugh at me now? Will I be the only one with eyeglasses?"

"You look great," said Crab.

"And we will not laugh," said Starfish.

"Yes, because now you will know who we are!" said Turtle.

"And you will not think that we are rocks or sea monsters!" said Dolphin.

"And you will see," Dr. O said, "that you are not the only one with eyeglasses!"

And now that Nan could see well, that is just what she did see!

"Well, what do you know about that!" said Nan.

Sharing the Joy of Reading

Beginning readers enjoy reading books on their own. Reading a book is a worthwhile activity in and of itself for a young reader. However, a child's reading can be even more rewarding if it is shared. This sharing can enhance your child's appreciation — both of the book and of his or her own abilities.

Now that your child has read **Nan and the Sea Monster**, you can help extend your child's reading experience by encouraging him or her to:

- Retell the story or key concepts presented in this story in his or her own words. The retelling can be oral or written.

- Create a picture of a favorite character, event, or concept from this book.

- Express his or her own ideas and feelings about the characters in this book and other things the characters might do.

Here is an activity that you can do together to help extend your child's appreciation of this book: You and your child can do this experiment to show how most people depend upon the sense of sight. Collect about a dozen small household items, such as a spool of thread, a measuring spoon, a crayon, and a coin. Without letting your child see the items, place them in a paper bag. Then ask your child to feel the objects without looking into the bag. After your child has identified as many of the objects as possible, remove them from the bag and compare how touching and seeing an object helps you to identify it.